Dreams

Margarita Robleda
Illustrated by Maribel Suárez

ALFAGUARA

Originally published in Spanish as *Sueños*
Adaptation of stories and songs to English: Georgette Baker

© 1999, Nidia Margarita Robleda Moguel

© This edition: 2004, Santillana USA Publishing Company, Inc.
2105 NW 86th Avenue
Miami, FL 33122
www.santillanausa.com

Managing Editor: Isabel Mendoza

Alfaguara is part of the **Santillana Group**,
with offices in the following countries:
ARGENTINA, BOLIVIA, CHILE, COLOMBIA, COSTA RICA, DOMINICAN REPUBLIC,
ECUADOR, EL SALVADOR, GUATEMALA, MEXICO, PANAMA, PARAGUAY, PERU,
PUERTO RICO, SPAIN, UNITED STATES, URUGUAY, AND VENEZUELA.

ISBN: 1-59437-842-8

Printed in Colombia

For Ximena Ballesteros Martínez

Hurry, little white horse,
time to come along!

Take me to the bright star
where my dreams come from.

2

On a great big boat,
I will sail away,

3

up over the rainbow,
where my new friends play:

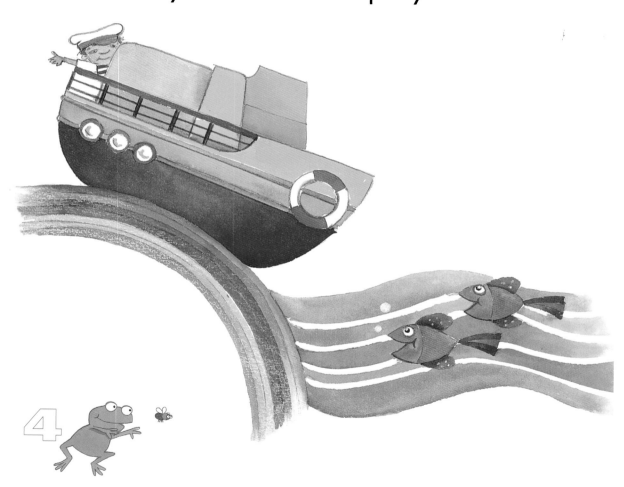

4

Dolphins, an octopus, and shrimp…

5

sea snails, fish, a chubby whale,

and a mermaid piñata with a fancy tail.

Hurry, little white horse,
race me past the farms

to the best place in the world...

zzzz......

9

my mommy's loving arms.

10

The Authors

Margarita Robleda likes to be called "Rana Margarita de la Paz y la Alegría" (Frog Margarita of Peace and Happiness). She is a Mexican writer who loves to play with words and use them to tickle her readers, both young and old. She has more than 75 published books. She also has books of riddles and tongue twisters in Spanish. In this collection, this frog rows and plays with rhymes, and her only wish is to make you smile.

Maribel Suárez was born in Mexico City. She studied Industrial Design and received her Masters in Design Studies at the Royal College of Art, in London, England. She has been illustrating children's books for about 20 years, and she enjoys it very much.